Published by Ad Hoc Fiction.
www.AdHocFiction.com

Purchasing Information:
Paperback available from www.AdHocFiction.com
E-book available from all usual outlets.

Printed in the United Kingdom.
First Printing 2020.

ISBN paperback 978-1-912095-81-0
ISBN e-Book 978-1-912095-80-3

This Alone Could Save Us

Santino Prinzi

For Mum, Dad, and Dario

For Matthew

Contents

When the Moon Distances Itself

The moon has been distancing itself from us because it misses our sense of wonder. The moon often reminisces about the days when we basked in its beams, when we would look up at it with appreciation, perhaps even admiration. Now we stare down at our phones and regard our neighbours with suspicion.

For a while, the moon has been creeping away, inch by inch, hoping we wouldn't notice its radiance dim. Somewhere between embarrassed and scared, it keeps an eye on us. Who can blame it? Look at what we're doing to ourselves. We're burning.

When we realise the moon is shifting away, we beg it not to go. We vow we can change. The moon listens, its crescent smile waning. It's not so confident in our words, but it remains still, it observes quietly.

The moon is confused. The moon doesn't know what to do.

Some people say we don't need the moon. They think it's for the best if the moon leaves. Murmurs float about that we should nuke the moon, that we should blast it to smithereens and see what the moon has to say then. People whisper it in all sorts of places: over the stalls of pub toilets, inside the doorways of failed businesses, while lounging across the polished benches of the houses of parliament.

Every night, those of us who want the moon to stay show it our love. We extend our hands up to the heavens to remind the moon that we're here. We chant, we sing, we dance, we offer feasts and throw parties, recite sonnets and rhymes. We measure how far away from us the moon has become, we keep checking if the space between us grows. But there's already so much space around us, so much history, and sometimes it's hard for us to know if we're becoming closer or if we're growing further apart.

A Confidence of Seagulls

The pier is quiet this afternoon. The sea shimmers below the creaky wooden boards. A seagull swoops and lands beside my hand and I pull my hand away. The seagull patters its feet on a metal table polished by vinegar and sea salt winds. I gulp down my surprise and gather the paper bag of warm doughnuts closer, licking the sugar on my cracked lips. It's the tastiest sting.

"You're not having these," I tell the seagull. I resist the temptation to shoo him off. I know the rules: you're supposed to comply, you're supposed to do what they tell you so you can diffuse the situation.

The seagull glares, like seagulls do.

"Gimme your wallet, mate."

My mother warned me before I moved away that the world can be an ugly place. The seagulls around these parts are confident. No-one's bothered about holding them accountable for what they do, so you have to do what you can to get by.

"Fine," I push the doughnuts away. I didn't fancy a fight. "Take them."

"Nah fam, don't mess."

Two more seagulls land on the railing beside the table. They puff up their white and grey chests, their piercing eyes darting, ready for an altercation. The red splodges on the underside of their beaks reminds me that adulthood isn't easy.

"We don't want no trouble," the second seagull says.

The third one says nothing. There's nothing more unbecoming than a silent seagull.

My mother warned me before I moved away that the world can be an ugly place. You've got to have your wits about you when it comes to men. Men and seagulls, they all want the same thing: they want what isn't theirs.

"I don't have a wallet," I lie, knowing the seagulls must've spotted me pull it out to buy the doughnuts. "Everything's cashless now, innit?"

"Give us your phone then," the first seagull says before checking the contents of the paper bag with its beak.

My mother warned me before I moved away that the world can be an ugly place. She taught me how to cope. This is how you manage your pennies. This is what you do when they call you a faggot. This what you do when a man tries to take something from you that isn't his to take.

I press the button on the switchblade and swipe at the first seagull, knocking my chair onto its back. The chair cracks the seascape with its metallic clang. The seagull jumps back, the paper bag dangling from its beak.

"Leave the doughnuts and fuck off."

The second seagull looks like he's about to do something stupid when the third holds up his wing, cocks his head thrice, and the other two fly away. He hops down onto the table, kicking the bag of doughnuts towards me, sniggering.

"The thing about bones is you forget you have them until they're broken."

The seagull plucks a feather from its wing and drops it into my hand. He flies off. I put the blade away and bite into a cold doughnut. Crossing the lilac clouds, the three gulls look serene, and the world doesn't seem like such an ugly place.

Splintered

His beard gives me a splinter during sex. He's inside me and all I can think about is how my finger is stinging and I need a pair of tweezers but I'm not sure if I have one. I yelp and suck my finger, but he mistakes this for a kink and carries on.

After he finishes, I hurry to the bathroom. He asks me if I'm okay and I tell him that if he used the beard conditioner I gave him for his birthday two months ago then I would be. He likes to keep his beard coarse; I like beards I can snuggle into and disappear.

I return from the bathroom with some tweezers and he's chewing on a Mars Bar. I ask if he has one I could eat because even sub-par sex makes me peckish. I know from the look on his face that he has one in his bedside drawer, but he fibs and says he doesn't.

I sit on the end of the bed and pull out the sharp grey stub of hair from my ring finger. I hold it there between the tweezer prongs. You can have this back, I say, offering him the hair. He asks me what

I expect him to do with it and I tell him that it's his beard hair, not mine, so it's his problem. I tell him that if he doesn't start using the conditioner I'll stop having sex with him because there's no way in hell I'm risking getting a splinter elsewhere.

He finishes the rest of his Mars Bar in one bite, opens his bedside drawer, and offers me the chocolate that I knew was always there.

Alright, he says. Alright.

Leaking

You open the front door and your husband is holding a toilet brush. It drips onto the carpet you had fitted three weekends ago. You hope it's not toilet water, you hope it's nothing worse. Your husband's name is Keith. You never thought of yourself as the sort of woman who'd end up marrying a Keith, but c'est la vie. The share bag of Dairy Milk giant buttons in your handbag is beginning to melt into one unwieldy chunk of gooey chocolate. It had been one of those days where you needed to come home to chocolate and an evening to yourself with no demands made of you. Both of you wait for the other to speak, and there's a hammering right behind your left eye. The toilet brush continues to drip, drip, drip. Keith's soaked clothes stick to his skin, the thinnest of trickles running from his trouser cuffs like he's leaking. You want to push past him and put your chocolate buttons in the fridge so they can solidify before it's too late, but there's no way you can't ask him why he's holding the toilet brush in the hallway and why he's so wet. You don't have the energy to hear him out. He blinks three times, slowly, silent, and you resist the urge to shake him into action. Instead, you uncurl his clammy fingers from the toilet brush and you take it from him. You think about kissing him but it's been too long since you've kissed him, so you don't. Bolting the bathroom door behind you, you sit on the toilet and open the share bag of chocolate buttons. They're molten enough to sticky and stain your fingers but solid enough to scoff. You scoop the delicious mess and devour it, smearing chocolate around your mouth while you roll your eyes at the brass seahorses you hung on the wall last July. You can't remember the last time you had sex, you can't remember the last time you felt as sensual as chocolate advertisers tell you to feel. It bothers you that it doesn't bother you. It bothers you how Keith is still dripping downstairs, seeping into the carpet, waiting for you to fix this mess. Sometimes you wish you could follow wherever the water flows, so long as it doesn't pool here. There's a wet patch on the back of your thigh but you keep eating, knowing there's only so many times you can ask something of someone.

It Sometimes Snows in April

December

Louise buys her fourth husband musical socks for Christmas. He's the most serious man she's ever married and he needs to lighten up. The socks are covered with disembodied snowmen heads and they play 'Let It Snow' whenever you press the musical speaker sewn inside. It'll be a laugh.

On Boxing Day, Edwin removes the musical speaker from the socks. He leaves them on the kitchen window ledge, either to be thrown away or repurposed. He liked to take things apart and put them together again, but Louise knows he won't reassemble the socks.

Whenever either of them opens the fridge, the speaker sings. They don't know why this happens, but she now knows whenever he's sneaking food before dinner and he now knows whenever she's pouring herself another glass of prosecco. They bicker about these deceptions into the new year, and it doesn't snow at Christmas.

THIS ALONE COULD SAVE US

January

The song haunts them at night. Louise wakes up on the first day of the new year determined to bin the musical device because the joke has turned on her. When she goes into the kitchen, the speaker is missing. She can still hear 'Let It Snow' playing from somewhere.

Her first instinct is to find Luna, their cat, who has a habit of taking things that don't belong to her. Louise expects the speaker to be caught around Luna's collar, but she purrs and rubs her head against Louise's shin before slinking away. If she's guilty of anything, it isn't this.

She searches under the sofa cushions, under the duvet and within her bedsheets. She even peeks inside the fridge. 'Let It Snow' continues to play from everywhere and somewhere, someplace she can't find.

"You've hidden it, haven't you?" she asks Edwin.

"No," he says, then turns up the telly.

Louise flips the switch in the fuse box, shutting the house down.

He asks her what she's playing at and she asks him what he's playing at hiding the speaker from the socks somewhere in the house just to wind her up.

"I haven't done anything," he says.

Over the next few weeks they keep their ears poised towards any chorus or verse from the Christmas classic.

February

On Valentine's Day, Louise apologises for accusing Edwin of hiding the musical speaker and he apologises to her for doing the same. They both stop looking for the speaker and spend most of the month sunbathing in the unseasonal heatwave.

March

The song weaves itself into normality. It rattles around the pipes, bumbles in the loft, and emerges from the garden daffodils in the spring. The lyrics appear in the rain droplet trails on the windows and wherever dust settles. They stir it into pasta sauces and roast it with potatoes and joints of beef. They snore the song in their sleep and sigh it during sex, moving with its rhythm. Soon, the lyrics replace 'I love you', and they sing the words to each other whenever there's an opportunity.

April

On their wedding anniversary, they dance and laugh around the living room, happier than they can remember. It shouldn't snow here in April, but snow is falling outside with an alarming urgency. Louise knows they should be worried about the snow, but instead she prays they'll never discover where the music is coming from. She hopes the battery never dies.

Full Circle

I stood and looked through the glass panels in the kitchen door into the living room where our cat, Balboa, laid on its side. Vomit and faeces stained the grey carpet, and I cried. My brother cried too, and he was five, so my mother lied and said *he's sleeping*. My mother scooped Balboa into a black bin bag because what else can be done, and that is where he sleeps. I didn't see it, but I know it's true.

We sat around the table in our kitchen, dinner was served. My brother and I were merciless. We would say *it stinks like wee*, or complain that it was too gloopy, or that we didn't know what it was, and my mother would say *it's nice*. We would cough and splutter, we would whine that we didn't want to eat leeks, we pushed our plates away, we spilled the gravy, we dropped glass and we never washed up. We were always told to eat our crusts so our hair would grow curly. *But I don't want curly hair, Mum*, though I did want to see in the dark.

Despite what I believed growing up, I learnt that I could do no better. I burnt rice to the bottom of pans, caught the tips of my fingers slicing carrots, was clueless when my dog died. I embraced my mother who, while criticising the floury lumps in the cheese sauce, ate the lasagne I cooked for her anyway.

When We Hit the Ground

Donna wheels her bike from the side of the old farmhouse then pedals. She doesn't want to cycle into the city to meet Claire for coffee. Couldn't they Skype?

Although the city wasn't far from the farm, Donna's sister kept her visits to the country to a minimum after she'd moved away. When their parents died, she stopped coming altogether, refusing to leave the safety of the concrete labyrinth for winding country lanes and fresh air.

It's early autumn. The foliage of the country is turning rusty and crisp, though few trees had yet surrendered their leaves. She looks forward to slowly enjoying the landscape later while cycling home at dusk.

Claire applies her lipstick in the reflection of her compact mirror: plum, seductive and authoritative. The coffee shop hums with bustling bodies, the scent of her Americano teasing her. She glances out the window. Donna's fifteen minutes late; probably stuck feeding some beast on the farm.

She pulls her MacBook out from her Cath Kidston bag; she can't afford to waste an entire day loafing around. Next week would be another busy one at work, but her weeks always are busy nowadays. The company is expanding and she isn't intending on being left behind. There are opportunities in London and New York. London would be close enough that Donna could still visit on the train, but she always dreamed of living in New York.

Donna is thirty minutes late now. Claire checks her phone. No messages, no missed calls.

The barista is flirting with two girls, and the girls are playing up to it, twirling their hair around their fingers, giggling. Claire hopes they're being ironic. They can't be older than nineteen and they're wearing matching outfits. She finds it nauseating.

"Lemme guess," the barista teases, "you're gonna order a Mocha frappe too?"

"Well, we are twins!" the girls say in unison.

Claire rolls her eyes. No, just no. She rarely tells anyone her sister is her twin because people assume nonsense like this, like they're telepathic or used to be conjoined. Though they are identical, even down to the freckles Claire smothers under foundation, she's her own person and not a reflection of another.

A white flash and a squawk. Claire swears she saw something flitter past the window. She tries to catch another glimpse of it but can't. The twins, who have noticed nothing, are both sucking on metal straws. An uneasiness stirs inside Claire. She packs up her things and leaves.

Donna's chest tightens. The roads are congested and streets are full of people – so many people – all rushing around. There's a commotion up ahead. People are swarming on either side of the pavement, cars are motionless but not silent.

Trapped in the middle of the road, flustered and unable to fly away, a swan cranes its neck, takes a few steps, then freezes before screeching and pacing in a different direction. Donna cautiously steps out into the road and tries to usher the swan onto the pavement or coax it into flying away. The swan unfurls its wings wide and shrieks at her.

"Go on," she flaps her arms. "Fly home!"

The swan glares at her with a beady eye. Her ringing phone vibrates in her pocket, sending tremors spiralling up her body. She doesn't answer it.

Years ago, she and Claire had left the back door of the farmhouse open and a swan had wandered into the kitchen. She remembers how they both tried to get the swan to leave before their mother found out, and Claire had managed to persuade the swan outside by trailing breadcrumbs.

"Donna?" Claire yells from the side of the road.

Screeching, the swan runs towards Donna while flapping its vast wings. She takes several steps back and shields her face with her arms. The motorcyclist weaving in and out of the stationary vehicles doesn't see her and they collide; the rider, Donna, and the swan all fly into the air amid the tangled sounds of car horns and scraping metal, but only two of them hit the ground.

Donna wakes up in a hospital with Claire sitting by her side. Save for a few machine bleeps and some muffled mutterings, the ward is eerily silent.

"Claire?" Donna sits up. "The swan?"

"It flew away."

"And the motorcyclist?"

"He's fine." Claire squeezes Donna's hand. "Count on you to risk your life for some stupid animal."

"Swans aren't stupid, they're graceful."

"Yes, graceful." Claire sees the freckles across her sister's face and smiles. "You're fine too, somehow; only minor fractures."

"What did you want to talk to me about?"

"No, now's not the time."

They sit in silence for a moment, not looking at one another.

"Do you remember when we were little and we'd left the back door open and that swan got into the kitchen?" Donna asks.

"I think so..."

Claire hadn't forgotten at all. It was her who'd saved the swan back then. They'd watched it soar into the sky together.

"Tell me then."

"Tell you what?"

"You wanted to talk to me about something."

"I – no, it's not important."

Donna squeezes Claire's hand and smiles.

Claire looks down at her lap. "Well, the thing is you see, the company I work for...There's some opportunities coming up... and, well..."

"New York, Claire. You have to go for it; you've always wanted to live there."

Neither of them speak; they both know what the other is thinking.

The Greatest Temptation of Mother Teresa

She tells us God works in mysterious ways, and we suppose she's right. That's how we're meant to explain the change we see happening in the world around us. But she also tells us that the devil has many guises, and he prefers exact change.

Her rosary beads in one hand, a vanilla ice-cream cone in the other, Mother Teresa shuffles away from the ice-cream stall. Drip, drip, drop, drip. Cold chastity seeps over the wafer edge, stickying her fingers. She licks the trickle, conflicted. She wants to waste nothing, but she's concerned about her actions being misconstrued by the Lord, by her fellow sisters. She'd hate to be thought of as naughty, even suggestive.

She looks around to see if anyone has seen her transgression. No, only Him. Forgive me, Father, for I have coveted and have succumbed to my sin. Again.

She'll pray for forgiveness, sucking her teeth for residues of deliciousness while thumbing her rosary beads.

The other sisters have always known of this pleasure she indulges, and they do not reproach her. They titter quietly among themselves about her little secret. Besides that, they don't care; they have their own virtue and vice to worry about. They know, too, that God's world cannot count for much if it's not to be enjoyed every now and then.

Black Sheep

Your stepmother's fridge is covered with magnets of sheep. Every kind of sheep imaginable, from plain photographs of sheep in fields to exciting three-dimensional cartoon sheep with googly eyes. You swear her fridge bleats when she opens the door. She collects the magnets for no particular reason; she just likes them.

You're convinced she's trying to hide the fridge from you. She knows you'll be raiding it for her not-so-well-hidden chocolate. The flock stare at you. If they could speak, they'd tell your stepmother that you ate her Cadbury's Fruit & Nut last week. Perhaps they already have.

Your dad comes into the kitchen and you whisper to him about the fridge magnets; you tell him they're getting out of hand. You ask him why she collects them and whether he knew about the magnets before he married her. Did they appear one-by-one, each a lone sheep lost in the woods to be saved from the wolves, or did they emerge from moving boxes as an entire flock?

He says something about loving Miriam despite her flaws and you want to ask him about your mother's flaws, the ones he couldn't love, the ones he chose not to love. You don't push it. Today's not the day to push it.

Miriam comes into the kitchen, suspicious. Her curly black bouffant is almost endearing, sheep-like. You'd love to shear her in the middle of the night to see how she'll react when she wakes. She tells you that she's plating up dinner in a minute so back away from the fridge. You offer to help her, hoping she'll say no. She looks from you to the Denby plates she saves for special occasions, then asks you to make some drinks for everyone.

After dinner, your dad brings out her birthday cake. Lemon drizzle, the only thing you're aware of that you can both agree on. There are two candles: one the number forty, the other a single number one placed to hide the zero so the candles read forty-one. Your stepmother blows them out, both of you knowing she's closer to fifty.

Miriam cuts the cake and asks if you'd only like a thin slice because you have your school prom coming up. You sneer into those small eyes of hers. There's nothing cartoonish about them, and you don't know what your father sees in her. You accept the thin sliver. Letting her win tastes wrong, so you only eat half the slice. It's not the best lemon drizzle you've ever tasted, and there's some solace in the hope that Miriam isn't enjoying it either. You thank her and excuse yourself, taking your plate through to the kitchen.

You see the cake box on the kitchen counter. It's from Waitrose, and you wonder when your dad started shopping there. The sheep on the fridge magnets glare at you. One is holding a meat cleaver, has excessive sideburns and a mullet, and is wearing a t-shirt that has "Mutton Chops" written on it in scarlet. There's something irksome about this magnet, like a joke that never lands. You pocket the mutton chop magnet, knowing that this is the closest you'll get to a victory today.

Dissolve

Unwrap the bath bomb, dip it into the steaming bath. Don't let it go. Don't let any of this go. Let the bubbles fizzle in your hand, let it dissolve through your fingertips. Hover your palm above the water. Gritty freshness catches beneath fingernails; you hope it never washes away. Count your breaths. Your eyes stream while you hold the bath bomb to your ears, ears once considered too small to hear sizzling. Step into the tub and smear the remnants of the bath bomb over your body; a body that's yours but not yours, a body you'll do something about soon, very soon. Dry your eyes first, then the body. Your father thinks he knows what you're doing in there and he's only half right. He says it ain't right for a man to spend so long in the bath. You don't correct his mis-gendering. He never listens. You sniff the air and smile. Six weeks until this humdrum town can fizzle through your fingers, until this man will deny all knowledge of your becoming. It all smells new like lemongrass and salt.

The Thingamajig

Whatsherface and Mateyboy are in the whatchamacallit sitting at the thingamabob. He asks her to pass the thingamajig and she remains silent. She's had enough of Mateyboy and his youknowwhat.

"Pass us the thingamajig," Mateyboy asks again.

Whatsherface takes another bite out of her thingamajigger, refusing to take her eyes off her gizmo.

He heaves a sigh. "Please? You know I can't drink my whatsitcalled otherwise. It won't taste right."

She's seen the thingys on his doodad. They hadn't had whatchamacallits in so long she'd stopped keeping track. Now she knew why. No, she'll pass him the thingamajig when he tells her everything about Whatshername.

"Please," he says again, "don't be unreasonable. Pass me the thingamajig."

She tries to remain focussed on her gizmo, wants to ignore him completely, but she can still see him in the periphery of her vision; a blurry gubbins bouncing around, demanding she look right at it.

Whatsherface had followed him last night to the doojigger, seen him with Whatshername. They had whatchamacallits for hours, laughing. Laughing at her, at how dumb she was, at how well they'd kept this going for so long without her finding out.

She grabbed the thingamajig, threw it at Mateyboy's wotsit, then left the whatchamacallit. She'd pack a dooberry and leave. She was tired of saying everything and nothing at the same time, tired of always tiptoeing around noughts.

Tessellation

Kerri wants to finish the puzzle, but there's a piece missing. She's made her own replacement, constructing it from cardboard Amazon packaging. It doesn't belong in the gap but she's forcing it in, bending the makeshift piece into this shape and that. She puts one edge of the piece into her mouth and lets her saliva swish and soak over the cardboard, her spittle rushing between her teeth, filling her head with squelching. The taste is disappointing, which meets her expectations.

She tries to fit the makeshift puzzle piece in the gap again. Something's lacking. She wedges it in, pounds it down with her fist. Please stay in place. Stay where she wants him to belong, where she needs him. Of course, it's not a perfect picture. These pieces don't fit together, and she's fully aware she doesn't need him to be complete, but she's not prepared to let go.

Keeping the Fires Burning

Whenever you visit your parents, your mother will be on her feet, ready to close the door behind you. She's become preoccupied with closing doors. It's her new thing. Your father's not concerned; he doesn't need to nag that she's letting the heat out like he used to.

You phone your sister and she's worried, but she's busy at work this week and every week before she holidays in Singapore. She rabbits on about this holiday for ten minutes, how she hasn't left the country in four months, how you can't possibly understand how difficult this all is for her, how she needs this break more than anything. You count the years it has been since you could afford a nice holiday. Seven? Eight? She hasn't even asked you how you're doing.

You decide to challenge your mother about this new habit she's formed. She says it's to keep the fires burning. You correct her, you tell her we keep doors closed to stop fires from spreading. No, Franz, she says, it's to keep the fires burning, and she doesn't break eye contact. You give in and look away.

You want to ask her about these fires, remembering her other habit of switching off all the electrical sockets from the wall whenever appliances weren't in use, her old habit of unscrewing lightbulbs from fittings in the summer months because who needs unnatural light in summer? When you were younger, she was a stickler for catching you not switching the kettle off, for leaving the bathroom light switched on, as if they were all conspiring against her, plotting her ruin.

You ask her if this door-thing has replaced the socket-and-lightbulb-thing. You ask her if she trusts the fridge-freezer not to explode. She reprimands you, tells you not to be silly, the fridge is fine – I am fine.

You need to get back to your husband and the little one. When you get up from the kitchen table to leave, your mother closes the door you tried to open and leans against it, not letting you pass. She isn't crying, but looks as if she may. She tells you she's trying to keep the fires burning, but she can't do it all by herself.

You think you get it because you've been trying to do something similar and it's so exhausting. You hold her, you help her keep the fires burning while your father knocks on the other side of the door, wanting to grab another beer from the fridge.

Some Feelings of Emptiness Feel Emptier than Others

It's 7:53am. I'm hungry and my breathing shallows and quickens. Other than a scattering of chocolate twists from yesterday, the pastry shelves are empty. I crouch, find a stray flake or two of crust, but there are no pecan slices.

Every morning my alarm chimes at 6:13am, even on weekends. It's loathsome but consistent. I've forgotten how it feels not to wake up disappointed. Are you writing this down?

People bustle past, baskets swinging. I buy pecan slices every day. I have one with a coffee when I get into the office, then one after my dinner-for-one in the evening. Should I buy the chocolate twists or find another shop? I can't... I don't know...

I have a goldfish called Freddy. He needs me. We share deep, meaningful conversations. Secrets. It's good to be relied upon, to know there's something living out there that needs me.

My life coach tells me to hold on to life's constants. I tell her that doesn't seem like good advice because it's all of the constants that are causing problems. She winces and writes something down. Everyone fancies that their life coach or therapist or counsellor never makes notes, only doodles pictures of cats or your imagined death. I know mine's drawing her evening: ratatouille, red wine, adequate candlelit sex with her husband on fake rose petals he's scattered and will gather into a plastic pot for their next planned moment.

...it's the most minor of all third-world problems, I know my issues aren't worthy, that they're trivial to you, I know you're all losing your patience with me, I know there are people being bombed, people being murdered because of who they are and because of who they love, people who board unsafe boats and cross seas to escape warscapes, who are faced with hostility if they're fortunate enough to hit land, and

I could be any one of those people but I'm not; what steals the breath from my lungs is the fact that there are no pecan slices, because pecan slices are one of my life's constants, one of the many things I'm trying to hold on to; I'm trying and trying, but I can't even hold on to breakfast...

It's not that I have a bad relationship with time, but time has a bad relationship with me. What's the word to describe how time passes both fast and slow, that nothing is changing for me but everyone else seems to be carrying on? To be winning life's lottery? It's a strange kind of emptiness, of loneliness, always being several steps behind. Time keeps ticking, keeps shortening. People never understand where I'm coming from. Do you understand me?

My life coach keeps writing, but she doesn't answer my questions. I don't even know if she's listening. Everyone just wants to be heard.

A woman who reminds me of Zoë Wanamaker says hello. She's wearing a maroon and orange fleece, which looks frumpy but warm. Her name tag says, 'Sandra'. She's holding two pecan slices in a plastic container. I can taste the fresh maple filling, can anticipate the crunch of the roasted brown pecans.

Here, she says. I take the pecan slices from her as I might a new-born child, and there's more than breath in my lungs.

My life coach thinks I need to change my perspective on everything. Nothing is ever as bad as it seems. I shouldn't focus on the years that slip by. Grab those moments between these repetitive constants that are waiting to be cherished, that are waiting for you to be present.

I think I need a new life coach.

Sandra says she knows I always buy pecan slices each morning, and when she saw me she went out back to the bakery to check if any were ready. I'm not listening to what she's saying. Her mouth is skipping, her eyes are full of glee, and I don't know what to say. This doesn't happen to people like me.

"Thank you, Sandra," I say and she beams warmth.

I stumble towards the self-service checkouts because I'm running late, then I stop. Sandra has returned to stacking loaves of bread on top of one another, checking dates as she goes, rotating stock. Her kindness is still glowing in her smile, but something dims while she returns to her shelving.

The percolator comforts me with its familiar sound, the smell of coffee beginning to fill the small office. There's only one pecan slice in the container and I've not eaten yet today.

Sandra's face blossomed with joy when I offered her one of the pecan slices. I keep replaying the moment in my head; the way she grinned like daybreak when she bit into the pastry, how she said yes when I asked her to dinner.

For the first time in a long time I don't feel so empty. It's a new feeling, not hunger, but not something unlike it. I feel full, so full that everything could overflow, could spill out and cascade from me, all over everything and everyone who comes near. I let it.

Showering

One of the shower curtain rings sits empty on the rail, the curtain having loosened itself. Your body is soap-sudsy and smells like ripe nectarines. The water is warm on your skin, and none of it is going where it shouldn't, but the slight lop-sidedness of the curtain bothers you. You stretch to hook the curtain back on its ring. You stretch further and slip, your hands reaching out to grasp anything that may stop your fall. You hear rips and pings, the ruffling up of the shower curtain as you tear it from the rail. It twirls itself around your body and you hit the bottom of the bath. You assumed that a white shower curtain would always look fresh and clean, but wrapped around your body you see the curtain for what it is: off-white and tinged with beige, black mould swarming around the edges. You hug the shower curtain like a blanket, staring up at the bathroom ceiling. The water remains constant, pattering your plastic quilt. You know you're fine, really, you know you're not physically hurt. You'll get up in a minute or three because you don't want to be late for the office. You lie there for a while and think about how you ended up here and it all comes back to you, how nothing's turned out the way you imagined. Even from this new perspective, even though the water is warm, you feel the cold creeping in.

Bleaching the Streets

Jean mops pigeon shit off the pavement outside the shopping centre entrance. It was her turn to mop it up, but then again it always is. The mixed sour odour of chemicals and shit will linger on her all day, resting like phlegm on her chest. Her apron and a pair of marigolds do nothing to protect her from the cold. Not even the boiling water helps.

Moving away from London to a smaller town was supposed to mean less shit to clean up. Life was supposed to get easier, though nothing ever does what it's supposed to do. If anything, it meant there was less of a crowd for her to lose herself in. It meant she stood out more.

Jean wishes she'd worn her winter coat, but it's one of her nicer items of clothing and she didn't want bleach to splash on it and strip it of its emerald glow. The chill sequesters deep inside her, burrowing to that place where people scrunch their dreams and ambitions into tiny balls and forget about them, leaving them to gather dust.

Wring, rinse, mop.

Bleach-spiked steam rises from the twist of her wringing, filling her mouth with a heaviness that makes her lick her teeth. There's a blustering overhead, a flappering. Two pigeons perch on the shopping centre's welcome sign. They coo, coo-coooooo.

Jean used to adore birds. She used to have parakeets. Whenever her grandparents took her to the zoo, she'd bypass all of the other animals and head straight to the aviary. Owls were her favourite. Peacocks, too. Though owls and peacocks were different birds in size, shape, and colour, there was something regal about them both that she aspired to. She wanted to be as majestic as those birds one day. Now, whenever Jean sees or hears a bird – any bird – all she smells is bleach. Bleach and shit.

She keeps mopping the pigeons' Jackson Pollock. She tells herself that she'll find a new job soon, but she can't imagine it being any different anywhere else. People always expect you to clear up their mess.

Her bus is late, as usual, and the line snakes across the station. She can smell bleach. A different bleach. She follows the scent towards the blue and white police tape cordoning off the men's toilets. The tape is upside-down and taut; there's no leeway for swaying in a breeze.

THIS ALONE COULD SAVE US

A policewoman asks her to step back, but Jean peers past her and through the toilet door. A person wrapped in white plastic from head to toe is mopping blood up from the floor. An alarming amount of blood. More blood than Jean believed a person could clean, more than she believed a person could hold inside them.

On the bumpy journey home, Jean promises herself that she's going to find her scrunched up ambitions, she's going to unwrap her dreams, watch them unspool into the world. She'll follow them wherever they go.

The Landmines Up Near Sapper Hill Sing

The day before we'd finished our stint de-mining the Falklands, Yousef lost his legs.

He knew the dangers, we all did, and it weren't as if he were taking risks. We all had experience of clearance projects like these, heard the stories, seen appendages blown to mist or found a few miles off. But this was Yousef's legs. Yousef's. The kindest heart in the group. S'way it always goes, though.

Six months after our stint de-mining the Falklands, Yousef and I are drinking in the Globe Tavern. Union Jacks and Falkland flags blazon the pub like a rash, bulging from the ceiling like stomachs. Slot machines whirr with an enthusiasm at odds with the punters. Some guy shoots pool, the clack of the balls making Yousef watch, making him winch slightly. He used to play before. Pretty good too.

"I'll play again soon," he says, knowing my thoughts. "I'll find a way to play when I'm used to this chair."

"Wan' another beer? I'm buying."

He nods.

The beer pump is shaped like a saxophone. So tacky, but also not. Today's dead. There's a chill outside that ain't shifting.

Up near Sapper Hill we tread along carefully mapped lines, not caring for the mud. We're each holding a corner of the square metal detector. Reminds me of a giant picture frame waiting to be filled. It should tell us where the mines are, where the thousands hide, Argentinian and British. The mines don't care who they maim, they know no better. I take a look around the barren field, knowing this place must've been beautiful before, that birds must've flown and sung joy.

I hear the detonation, and I don't see the man I've quietly loved all these years.

I set Yousef's beer on one of those coasters that soak up the condensation, those coasters you pick the colour off once it's damp. He gulps half of it down without a breath.

"Steady on, fella."

He wipes his unshaven face on his fleece sleeve.

"You know, I wouldn't change anything." He glares at me, like he needs me to say something

I can't. "We used to say it all the time, didn't we? Every time we found a mine and sorted it out, that's a life we've saved. Didn't we used to say that, Glynn?"

"We did," I say, and we both drink deep.

Because We All Need the Snow

Each snowflake is individual, everyone knows. You know snowflakes are made of ridges and grooves, ribs, rimes, and rockets. No-one can see them, but you like believing in unseen things. You have faith that each snowflake has a little mouth and a tiny pair of ears. They speak to you. They listen. You could politely request a blizzard and they'd invite everyone they know. You go outside and ask them, holding your palms open. You catch a few snowflakes on your gloves while others dissolve on the ground. You murmur to your snowflakes, in those little ears you believe in, and you ask them to try harder. Please, try harder, because you need them to smother everything they can see through those bulbous eyes you're certain they have. You know these snowflakes can do it, you know their strength. You want your kids to open their bedroom curtains this morning and see that the world is glistening, that the world can glisten. You believe that these snowflakes, if they have miniscule brains and hearts, would understand this isn't for you but it's for the kids. You hope the snowflakes spread the word, you pray the snow spreads itself thick, hiding the truth for a day or two. Yeah, for the kids.

Smoke Detectors

There's the bleep again. My father knows it's one of the smoke detectors but he can't figure out which one. It started crying two hours ago. He's roaming around the house, head cocked to the ceiling, carrying an old collapsible chair. The fake leather seat is torn and the cheap sponge padding springs out from it like it has someplace else to be.

I cannot sleep, the smoke detector says.

Neither can we, we tell it.

Bleep. Not the kitchen, my father shouts before heading to the next room. Our lives are full of rooms we've stood and waited in.

Safety isn't something my father risks, but there's only so much you can do. He once told me he knew someone who'd died in a horrible fire, who'd had no smoke alarms, whose bedroom door wouldn't open, how the same charred door had bloody grooves where he'd clawed at it in desperation, their fingers digging into solid wood. He told me this when I was four years old so I'd stop striking matches and dropping them down the side of my mattress because I liked watching the fire fall. Sometimes I think he made this story up to scare me. Sometimes he gets twitchy around birthday candles. He believes birthdays count down rather than up.

I overhear the smoke detector on the landing ask my father if he misses his wife.

Bleep.

Not the landing. He knocks, comes into my bedroom, and listens. If he didn't find it soon, he'd make me lend him an ear. He's paranoid about being hoodwinked; he doesn't want to waste a new battery.

Bleep. My bedroom is fine.

Would you mind, Lucie?

I carry the chair and follow him around the night, silent, waiting. He has a good feeling about the one in his bedroom, a gut instinct.

The smoke detector smiles feebly, caught wiping away its tears.

I'll sleep soon, I promise, I haven't much left to give.

Bleep.

I unfold the chair and my father climbs up, opens the smoke detector's chest, and withdraws its heart. This isn't forgetting, my father tells the smoke detector, it's impossible to forget.

When given the new battery, the smoke detector screams and my father wobbles on the chair and nearly falls. I grab him, steadying him like my mother would've done. I've got you, I say, and through the smoke detector's wail we hold each other. I've got you too, he says, I've got you.

Nonni
In loving memory of Gregorio Prinzi

Nonno's snoozing on a dining chair he's hauled out to the front garden. Tweed cap and cane; a statue, jacketed. He's smiling a little; in his dreams, he's dancing to a tarantella. I gently wake him. Eyelids flutter into a twinkle. His voice is low and welcoming as usual. A glint catches my eye. Nonno's holding his harmonica; I haven't heard him play in years. I let myself inside the house and tell him to keep enjoying the sunshine because rain is coming.

Nonna's cooking in the kitchen. Cannelloni. Always smelt before seen. Your favourite, she says, and she pulls out a chair. There's a bag of red striped greasy pole beans on the seat. I remember carrying a bag of them like this one from the allotment for Nonno, my brother and I helping Nonna shell them in the evening. I slip one into my pocket as I move the bag. If Nonna sees me do it, she doesn't protest. Nonno shuffles into the kitchen as Nonna opens the oven door, as if he already knew lunch was ready. I devour a plateful and Nonna insists I have more. *Eat! Eat!*

After lunch, Nonno returns to the sun and I insist in washing up for Nonna. She won't listen. She tries to smush a fiver into my palm. Our hands flitter, each refusing ownership of the money. Gesticulations, how Italian. Nonna follows me outside when I leave. Nonno is still sitting in his chair, soaking up the sun. Nonna stands behind him, her hand on his shoulder, and the smell of pasta sauce lingers about them both.

When I get home, I sit in my car and wait. I stare in the rear-view mirror, then at the petrol gauge. It's nearly empty. I take the red striped greasy pole bean from my pocket, peel away its shell, and eat the bean raw. I close my eyes and Nonno is sitting in the sun, playing his harmonica. I wish I'd taken their photograph.

It starts to rain, but there are places the rain will never reach.

A Wristwatch Can Measure More than Time

Nestled in a pile of dead leaves, a wristwatch with a verdant face catches the mid-afternoon sunlight. It's not mine to take, but I pocket it anyway. It's probably worth something.

A spider with seven legs perches inside my favourite mug. It's so spindly that a breeze could lift it out of this world; I wish it would. I haven't cleaned any of Trev's dirty mugs and dishes. He promised he'd wash them when he came back and I'm still waiting. The kettle finishes its boil and I want to scald the spider, but this isn't the spider's fault, and a spider with seven legs has been through enough already. We've both been through enough.

I put the wristwatch back on the pile of dead leaves. No, I shouldn't take what isn't mine, and I wouldn't wear it anyway.

Does he remember these woods from our picnics? We went for one during the summer of the EU referendum. There was an unseasonable chill and we argued about how much space I was taking up on the blanket. Everything that summer was about space and who had the right to occupy it. Trev removed the wristwatch I'd bought him, his wrist cuffed by a pink sweat rash, and he placed it on a pile of leaves. I told him the juxtaposition of the natural and manmade was beautiful; he smiled and nodded. He kissed me while thunder growled overhead. We ran for the car, tumbled inside, fumbled all over each other. We laughed ourselves breathless and we both forgot about the wristwatch.

He never cleaned his mugs or dishes. I waited for Trev for three weeks before I gave in. Even the spider had left. I checked the corners of the kitchen for it. I never found out if it regrew its missing limb. I like to think it did, I like to think you can replace a part of you someone else has taken.

Trev's not coming back, so I take the wristwatch I bought him for his birthday, brush off the crispy leaf flakes. No matter how I fasten it, its grasp is either too tight or too loose, which seems about right.

Towels

My mother stuffs the vases in her house with towels so nothing can crawl inside them. She places towels on every chair cushion to stop germs transferring from the seat to her bottom and then, somehow, inside her body. Whenever I visit, there are always towels duct-taped to the window panes to block out sunlight, to stop people peeping in as they bumble past. Sometimes the towels sway in the draft.

I try to visit twice a week, sometimes more. I peel the towels from her windows, stripping more paint and plaster from the walls each time, whip the towels off her chairs, un-stuff her vases.

She's silent while I do this. From room to room she follows me, memorising where each towel came from. When I've found every towel, she hobbles away to put the kettle on. I fold the towels and pile them at the end of her bed, refusing to count them as I go. I know there'll be more than last time.

Afterwards, I find her sitting in front of the telly in my father's old armchair with a cup of peppermint tea. It makes the room smell like stale toothpaste. She never offers to brew me any.

Somehow she's sitting on a towel, one she's kept hidden for emergencies. She asks after my ex-wife like Davina's still living with me, asks where my now adult sons are. I wish I knew. I lie through the sound of EastEnders repeating.

My mother's neighbour wants to know what the deal is with the towels. He says it's unnerving and ill-fitting of the neighbourhood image. I point at his begonias, tell him they're drooping, and leave while he's distracted, fearing the day I visit my mother and can see clearly through her window panes that she's finally forgotten everything.

Relinquish

Erza and Zig stand on the edge of the jetty, craning their necks up. The blood moon looms in the sky like a copper coin, its reflection smudged across the shimmering lake. Ezra quakes, tiny little shakes all over his body. Warmth ripples through him. His heart pounds, hope catches in his breast. He shuffles a little closer to Zig, the boards beneath his feet moaning. His hand swings gently, bumps against Zig's fingers, even though the air is still. Zig doesn't look away from the moon.

If this was a particular kind of story, they'd take their clothes off and go swimming. They'd see each other's bodies glisten in the water. They'd laugh and frolic, then emerge from the lake fresh and freezing. Naked or in their underwear, their vision of each other would be complete and deliberate – no stolen glances when t-shirts rise while the body stretches. They would see their muscles and scars and limbs and moles and birthmarks and dimples and they'd fall in love. They'd touch, they'd understand who they are, that they've not only been fighting against the world but also themselves. They'd give up that fight and kiss, they'd lie on the jetty under the moon wet from sweat and lake water, they'd press against each other. And then something will change, something bad will happen because every gay love story is filled with tragic undertones, because God forbid that anyone should be happy. But this isn't that kind of story.

Ezra wants Zig to forgive him for their petty arguments. He thought that taking him to their favourite spot under the moon when it looks mesmeric like it does tonight would make this place even more special to them both. Zig thinks about the moon, how they say the moon is moving away from the earth, a slow, gradual retreat. He thinks about what would be lost if the moon were to disappear, how ordinary the sky might be without it. Zig takes Ezra's hand and squeezes.

How to Make the Magic Work

I was seven when my mother first showed me how to make the magic work. She told me to wear an elastic band around my wrist and ping it every time I had a bad thought. I asked her about good thoughts and bad thoughts and how you're supposed to tell the difference. She pinged my elastic band. She pinged it hard.

"You know the thoughts, Adam, you know which thoughts I'm talking about."

She said to me that if I was in any doubt I should ping the elastic band anyway. It will only do me good.

The elastic band blended in with my arm. One morning, before school, I dangled my wrist in front of my mother and showed her how it looked like a bracelet. She grasped my arm and pulled me to her side and hissed at me to stop being so queer, to stop talking such nonsense, that boys don't wear bracelets. Then she pinged the elastic band three times.

Try as I might, I couldn't get the magic to work. The bad thoughts kept coming and I stopped telling my mother about them. I sat in my bedroom for hours by myself, snapping the elastic band.

When I was eleven I added a second band, then a third. I would ping them all together, all at the same time, and my wrist was permanently marked with a red ring made smooth by years of elastic snagging my dark hairs.

My mother grimaced whenever she looked at my wrist because she knew the magic wasn't working, but she had faith in the Lord.

"One day the bad thoughts will disappear," she promised. "You'll find a nice girl and you'll get married and have children and everything about this will be dead and gone, trust me. You just have to keep snapping those bands."

When she dies, I snap the elastic bands for days. I wedge myself in the corner of her front room and stretch my body across the carpet. I keep her curtains drawn, I leave the knocking on her front door unanswered. There's nothing they can say, nothing I can do; the bad thoughts hold me down, they fall heavy and unwelcome all around me like unexpected snow.

Snap, ping, snap, ping, snapping, snapping, snapping.

Enough. I push the bad thoughts off me, get up, and run. I keep running until I'm breathless. There's water gushing and I'm on a bridge. The river beneath is grey from the sludge of discarded things: crisp packets, plastic bottles, trollies, thoughts and feelings. There has been so much rain this past month that the rivers waters are wild and high. They could grab me, take me wherever they wanted. Everything thrown in the river must end up somewhere.

The bad thoughts find me. They grasp my scarred wrist and wait for the next ping. I hear her, my mother, but I can't make out what she's saying. She's in the water, she's shaking her head. I move a little closer to the edge of the bridge and ready myself to ping the elastic bands.

They break. They come away in my hand. I hold them up to the moonlight, three feeble brown worms, dead and powerless. My wrist feels light and something is different, like the earth beneath my feet has somehow shifted, like a spell has been cast over me and I'm enchanted by this weightlessness.

I throw the broken elastic bands into the water. I don't watch to see where the river takes them.

This Way Around

You both look away and grimace, but I keep
looking at the TV, hoping you're not watching
me watching them. There's a welling up inside
me, the sensation of sneezing and trying not to,
while nervous sweat seeps down my back. Look.
Look away. The men are playing scrabble because
they're trying to abstain from sex, but they scatter
the board, the letter tiles, and their bodies across
the floor. They're making a language of their own.
The TV programme we're watching is about a man
who'd divorced his wife because he was in love
with another man. Or is it the other way around?
It's new, seeing what I'd always felt was so wrong
seem so right. Dad says he's lost respect for those
actors. Mum is silent. I can't stop thinking that
none of this is normal and I never will be.
        No-one should have to put up with this.
    I can't stop thinking I am normal and this soon
    will be. Mum is silent. Dad says he's lost respect
        for those actors, but so fucking what? It's new,
    knowing what I'd always felt was so wrong become

so right. It's definitely this way around. The TV programme we'd watched was about a man who'd divorced his wife because he was in love with another man. The men played scrabble because they were trying to abstain from sex, but why abstain from love? They scattered the board, the letter tiles, and their bodies across the floor. They inspired a language of their own, inspired me to speak. Don't look away. Look. There's a welling up inside me, the sensation of sneezing and trying not to, while sweat seeps down my back. You both look away and grimace, but I keep watching the TV, smiling quietly to myself, thinking about him – the one I've quietly been smitten with.

Upon Discovering that Cows Can Swim

You're on a boat on Lake Nicaragua. A tour. Your reflection in the water is murky, like a shadowy chartreuse-coloured twin staring up from beneath the surface. You want to touch her, your twin, but you don't. You're always refraining. That's when you hear their breathing, and you're not the only one. Others on the boat have spotted the cows grazing on floating foliage. You look up to see another cow swimming down the creek. She looks majestic, graceful, her horns sharp and glistening. You want to fashion a wreath from wildflowers and crown her. The captain conducting the tour says cows are his favourite animal and he rubs his stomach. You spy the stomach hanging from beneath his t-shirt, that reddish-pink of flesh peeping from polyester. There's nothing friendly about this. The others laugh at his jokes while you contemplate veganism. The swimming cow rests with the others and grazes. You watch, knowing this is the most unusual thing you'll see on this trip. When you have signal on your phone, you'll google to check if cows can swim because you need to know if something this marvellous is real. Because you need to know that something so marvellous can be real.

Bonsai and Clyde

Clyde is in love with his houseplant, Geraldine. It's an ill-fitting name for a bonsai tree but he's sure she'd have changed it if she'd wanted to. On the kitchen window ledge, she sits overlooking their south-facing garden. She's happy, he's sure of that.

Houseplants wouldn't usually stick around long enough for Clyde to get to know them on a first name basis. They'd wither into themselves, dropping their bright flourishes into overwatered soil or crisping into brittle, dry-rooted ruins. But Geraldine wasn't like the other houseplants: Geraldine stayed.

Geraldine won't tell Clyde what kind of Bonsai she is. He googles her, tries to find her on Facebook or Twitter. He tries to find pictures of other bonsai trees who look similar to her, but none quite resemble his love. She refuses to have her picture taken because she doesn't want him flaunting her on Instagram like some trophy hashtag. She wants to keep their relationship a secret until they've been going steady for a little longer because this thing they've got going on is all new. He respects her wishes, but imagines a time when he can shout his love for her in the streets.

While he waters Geraldine, Clyde tells her that her foliage is enchanting. He sighs that she's so sturdy yet delicate as he strokes her bark. She's not in the mood for his nonsense today. She says he only loves her because she hasn't died on him like the others. All night she winds him up and relishes in it.

They were always fooling around like this, playing tricks on one another, fighting over who would have the last laugh. Clyde knew Geraldine would've been the kind of woman who'd pick the glacé cherries from cherry bakewells and eat them, leaving him to discover the cakes in their box, cherryless, the best bit stolen. But she isn't, she's a plant, yet that night she keeps him chuckling until she falls asleep in his arms. He'd forgotten what moments like this felt like. It had been such a long time.

In the morning, Clyde asks Geraldine if she'll flower for him. She wilts slightly, stays quiet. I can't have flowers, she says, and he apologies, but Geraldine doesn't speak to him for the rest of the day.

Clyde stands in the garden centre, deliberating over which plant pot will be enough to make amends. Indecisive, he instead searches the shelves for another bonsai like Geraldine, but he still can't find anyone like her.

He wipes his eyes on his coat sleeve and picks up a fuchsia and yellow paisley patterned pot; he's sure she likes those colours. In the light, the yellow is sometimes gold, sometimes sunshine. He looks around for a member of staff or a CCTV camera, then slips the pot into the canvas bag he'd brought with him. Yes, she'll love this. These must be her favourite colours.

When he gets home, he asks Geraldine to close her eyes. She obliges, chattering away about having to do so much housework. She asks him if he's given the energy company the electric and gas meter readings like he promised? Clyde hushes her, says he'll sort everything out, that everything has been a little much lately but he'll get back on top of things soon. The thin tissue paper rustles in his hands while he unwraps Geraldine's present, and he shows her the new pot he'd bought her. May I? he asks, and her leaves quiver in approval.

He tries to remove Geraldine from her pot but she won't budge. He's sure she's winding him up again, so he applies a little more force and he drops her. She doesn't cry out in pain, she doesn't break. There are no fallen leaves, no soil spread across the kitchen floor. Instead, she bounces.

Clyde lies beside the plant, quietly laughing to himself, then he starts crying. This time she's gone too far. This was against the unspoken rules of their game. The tears keep coming and he decides he isn't going to get up from the floor until they stop.

When she was dying, his wife Geraldine had told him that he'd need to look after all the houseplants for her, that this would keep her memory alive. One by one they'd all died on him, except the bonsai.

He wished he listened to everything else his wife had said. He wished he'd listened to her ramblings about home décor and plastic houseplants. Then he'd have known that he'd never have the last laugh. He can see her now, sitting at the kitchen table, looking over him, her hair overflowing with auburn curls, her eyes full of laughter while she eats a cherryless bakewell.

Palm Lines

You visit the palm reader because you crave instruction and you have no-one left who will tell you what to do. The palm reader sits in a room heavy with incense. She doesn't have a wart or a hook nose, giant hoop earrings or papery skin. She looks, if anything, like a model from a clothes catalogue. You can see her now, being photographed on a white sandy beach, not quite knowing what to do with herself, used to giving direction instead of taking it, but somehow still being hypnotic.

The palm reader takes your hands, turns your palms skyward, and traces your lines with her fingers. Rosewater emanates from her, swimming through the incense and tickling your nose hairs. You refrain from sneezing, unsure how this could affect your fate. The palm reader starts picking at the dead skin below your ring finger. You'd prefer she didn't, but you've never done this before and maybe it's all a part of the authentic palm reading experience. It doesn't hurt, so you let her continue to do her thing.

Your palm line comes loose from beneath your skin like the frayed edge of a jean hole, the knees worn through. You haven't prayed in years because God's done listening. She hesitates, her breathing heaving under the weight of the night, then asks if you mind. You tell her to do what she has to do, and you wonder if this has ever happened with anyone else before.

She gently tugs and plucks, twizzling the palm lines around her left hand like red twine. The palm lines stain her finger tips, and a handful of blood droplets speckle the tablecloth. It tickles. You want to giggle but you suppress the urge because the palm reader doesn't look amused. You need her to take you seriously, to take your future seriously. You want to ask if everything's alright, even though you both know that's why you came here in the first place. You hope she knows that's why you came here.

She holds your palm lines to the candle's light, then she stretches them on the table. She spreads them out like pieces of a puzzle she's trying to work out, like socks she's trying to match. You ask her what this all means and she shushes you. Her face is so close to your palm lines you wouldn't be surprised if she licks them. She glares at you for too

THIS ALONE COULD SAVE US

long, says there's nothing she can tell you that can prepare you for what's to come. The last thing you remember is your inverted reflection in her crystal ball, your whole world turned upside down.

At home, you lay your hands on the dining table and study your palms. If you knew how to read them yourself, you would have a choice. You could follow the destiny mapped out on one palm, or you could follow your blank palm, directionless and full of possibility. Literate in the art of palm reading or not, you still have a choice to make, and your palms are staring back at you, waiting.

This Alone Could Save Us

As we buckled up, I promised my paranoid boyfriend that nothing bad would happen.

"You're more likely to die in a car accident than a plane crash, especially the way you drive."

"Perhaps you're right," he said, "but if our plane does decide to plummet back to earth, that's it. Boom. Bye."

"But it won't; the odds are in our favour."

Three hours later and we were in the dark, oxygen masks hugging our faces, clutching onto each other, ignoring the commands to – BRACE! – BRACE! – unable to share those final words over the shrieking. Unable to share a final kiss. And yet, underneath his obvious horror, there was an 'I told you so' look on my boyfriend's face.

This was not how I wanted him to remember me, not how I wanted to remember him in these last moments. We were going to die in a spiralling tin can and now wasn't the time for an argument over who was right.

Against his will, I let him go and scrambled in my rucksack. If he was going to have the last word, it might as well be a one that mattered. I pulled out a notebook and pencil and scribbled.

Either through fear or elation, he cried and grabbed me tight me as if this alone could save us.

The plane levelled out, the lights returned to normal, and the screams subsided into cheers and clapping, laughter and relief. The captain announced that we'd be making an emergency landing at the nearest airport. We were headed in a different direction.

My boyfriend couldn't contain his excitement. He was telling everyone seated around us about our news, anyone who would listen. He grinned when the captain announced our engagement and shared her well wishes. I forced enthusiasm but remained in my seat, quietly gripping the underside of my seat. He started planning the wedding breakfast menu, the venue, what song the string quartet would play when we danced our first dance. He was asking me how the ceremony itself would work, which one of us would walk down the aisle, would we have best men if the best men in our lives was surely each other. All I could think about was everything that'd just happened, that we could've been ash and cinders instead of debating wedding favours. I fanned myself a little with the sick bag.

My boyfriend beamed at me and his eyes brimmed with love. My perfect engagement plans scheduled years from now melted into his arms. I knew this wasn't the right time for us – for me – but there was no way I was going to tempt fate by calling things off. I kissed his hand and braced.

You Lost Something in Your Earthquake that You'll Never Get Back

In the Spotlight
Dad texts, "There's a programme on TV about your earthquake." It wasn't mine, and I don't want it. Spotlights don't swing like lampshades, but I stare at them all the same, waiting for them to move.

Foreshocks
The hotel wobbles, the lampshades sway. "Did we just?" I ask my friend.

The Ground is Deafening
Nine storeys. A coffee shop in a department store. Never have I heard the ground roar like this. Glass crashes. People dive under tables, shroud their heads with limbs. Lampshades pendulum. I wait, certain that the earth will disappear beneath my feet, but it doesn't.

SANTINO PRINZI

Sea Vortex
A tsunami is coming. Everyone files out of the building politely, side by side. No-one will remember the whirlpool; they'll only speak of the great wave. It takes an hour and a half to walk from Ikebukuro to our hotel in Shinjuku. Everyone is orderly, calm. Keep to the left of the pavement. People talk and I'm happy not to understand Japanese. Sometimes there are things you don't need to know.

You Cannot Stop the Water
It will always flow, even where you don't want it to, when you don't want it to, claiming what doesn't belong to the sea as its own.

Something Nuclear Shifts
I ask Dad, "Will I die?" because Fukushima is melting. The ground tremors. "No, I promise," he types after purchasing expensive plane tickets on a credit card. In my heart, I know something in me has.

Meltdown
When Mum wakes up to the news, she screams and screams and screams.

Aftershocks
I'm lying in bed. Dad wants to know if I'm coming
downstairs to watch this programme or not. I turn
off the lights so I cannot see if they tremble.

Utskjæring

Three months after I move to Norway, my sister turns up at my front door unannounced. Bridie tells me there's no place she'd rather be. She's lying; she wouldn't go near a cold climate unless she needed something.

She wants to hear me play the cello again. The last time she heard it – the last time we saw each other – had been our mother's funeral.

I recommend a few songs she can stream online and she puts her foot in the doorway, tells me not to close it. Our mother wouldn't want this, so I invite Bridie in.

I offer her some leftover beef stew and dumplings and she refuses. She's vegan now. I chop up and dry fry an aubergine, boil some rice.

"If you wanted something more exciting, you should've told me you were coming."

"If I'd have told you," she says, "you'd have run away again."

I keep my cello in my bedroom. I like knowing it's in the same room as me while I sleep. Sometimes I lay the cello on the bed and spoon it into my dreams. I take it out its case and hold it, stroke the polished wood, and slowly brush the strings with my fingertips.

There's a glistening at the bottom of the case. I pick up my mother's brooch and fiddle with its clasp. It's the only thing I have of hers. It's an iridescent peacock – emerald and sapphire and gold.

Bridie knocks on the door, giddy, and asks if I'm about to play something. I put the cello and the brooch away. The longer I keep her waiting, the more agitated she'll become.

"How long are you planning to stay here?" I ask.

"I'm going to have a shower, where do you keep your towels?"

The next morning, I tell Bridie I'm going for a walk to clear my head and that there's only one set of keys for the house, so if she leaves before I come home she'll be locked out. She bites her unbuttered toast.

Snow crunches underfoot as I walk through the forest. I close my eyes and follow the scent of solitude and pine; my feet know where I'm going. I arrive at the base of the mountain where the snow cave is being sculpted. A giant igloo, large enough to contain a stage and seating. I can't help but warm to it.

No-one else is here. I hum the music I've been rehearsing for next week's concert. I sit on a boulder while positioning my arms as if I'm holding my cello, and I pretend music is drifting through me, from me. No matter what happens or wherever I go, I'll always have music.

Bridie asks me about the concert of ice and I ask her how she found out. She says she went out for a walk in the town this morning and saw a poster in a coffee shop window.

"So, those instruments are really made of ice?"

There's nowhere in this kitchen to hide.

"Yes," I say, "they carve them out of ice."

"How?"

"Chainsaws."

"Chainsaws?"

"Chainsaws, mostly. Then they're finessed."

"Wow."

She opens the fridge and pulls out some orange juice, drinks straight from the carton. She wipes her mouth on her sleeve. "Don't they ever melt, these instruments?"

THIS ALONE COULD SAVE US

I look outside and watch the snow fall.

"I mean from friction or body heat. Surely the concert cave or whatever it's called gets a bit too cosy?"

I couldn't be bothered to explain to her how the snow cave is designed so the hole in its roof pushes all the hot air out, keeping the cave as cold as possible.

"I guess I'll have to find out for myself," she says.

"You're not coming." My lower back twinges and my temples ache. "Anyway, it's sold out."

Bridie hops off the breakfast bar stool and pulls out a ticket from her back pocket. She flaunts it, taps it against her palm.

"Fine," I say, "but afterwards you can leave."

On the night of the performance, I wear my mother's brooch on my scarf so it's not hidden beneath my layers. It was the only way I could take a little piece of her to Norway with me, is the only way she can listen to me play my music again. I know somewhere she's listening.

I see my sister creep in right before the show is about to start. She gives me a little wave but I don't reciprocate. This moment isn't for her.

The ice cello is cold in my gloved hands, but light shines through its glacier body and into mine. I hear my mother's voice reverberate from the ice cello's strings. She always used to sing. I caress the surface of the cello. Everything is still and somehow moving. I can hear the music fill the air and I can see my hands moving; they're creating music that's fluid like water, determined like ice, soft like snow.

I know she's here. I touch her brooch and she's here.

Bridie says the concert was magical, that I was magical. We embrace for the first time in years, my mother's brooch pressing between us. We're all together again.

I wake up at noon the next day, much later than usual. I follow the smell of toast and coffee. A mug and a plate have been washed up and left to dry alongside the wine glasses and the empty bottle Bride and I shared last night.

I knock on her bedroom door, then let myself in.

Bridie isn't there. Her clothes and suitcase are gone, her bed is made. It's as if no-one has ever been here. I didn't think she'd leave without saying goodbye.

I go back to my bedroom to make my bed and realise my mother's brooch is missing, that my sister has got what she came for.

Her First Honeymoon

The pebble beach forced Esther to teeter across the stones. Their blazed skins prickled her feet. She'd stretched a black vintage swimming costume over her pregnant body and held her wide-brimmed sunhat in place because of the strong winds. She felt the part, glamourous even, as if the cameras were rolling while she hobbled towards the ocean. Arthur lounged on a towel and watched her bobble in the waves; he was ready to spring up and catch her if she started to drown. On the seascape, a boat rocked violently and made the water look angrier than it was. As she rode the waves, Esther stared at her husband through winged sunglasses and wondered if it was enough to measure love by good intentions.

Getting the Gang Back Together

We bump into each other, feigning surprise at this reunion on the declining high street. We say it's been such a long time, we ask how the other is doing, and we pretend we're interested in what the other has to say. We force ourselves to find more things to talk about – weren't we such great friends? – and then we agree that we will have to get the gang back together for a drink sometime. We always agree to get the gang back together, but what we really mean is: you organise it. We both know neither will. I say we could go to the pub we used to always go to; the one where you and the others used to buy drinks for me because I was a summer baby; the one where Khloe slapped that man who grabbed her tit. Remember when Liam stepped in a shit that he didn't see on the bathroom floor? We laugh and we laugh, but it's different now; the pub is filled with chavs, the drinks are twice the price and watered down, the food is microwaved, and the carpet looks like it'd give you the clap. You suggest a new place. That'll be a great idea, I say, and we reaffirm our commitment to get the gang back together. But there isn't any gang left: Khloe lives in the States, Liam's in prison, and we're the only two stuck in a town that always smells like sewage. I say that I'd best let you get on, that you must have things to be getting back to, and we both know that's true. You're married, you have a job, and you have to pick up your son from playgroup – doesn't time fly? You and I both know that I'm the one who has nothing left – no reason to stay in town, no means to move away. We leave, and there's nothing I want more than to get the gang back together, but it's never going to happen.

Some Supernatural Force

Momma thinks I'm watching the ghost show on TV with her because I love the paranormal like she does, but I'm actually in love with the presenter. It's a quiet, secret love. It prickles my toe tips, makes the walls of my stomach tingle.

He's in a hotel. It's haunted – obviously – but this room is special. This room has had the most reported paranormal activity. The wallpaper is peeling, and the curtains are raggedy and covered in a flowery-beige pattern. The bed bends beneath the presenter's weight as he stretches across the bed, his midriff showing, the mattress almost touching the floor.

He says the ghost in this hotel grabs people – grabs women – and whispers things to them that they don't wanna hear. I know what the ghost would tell Momma. He's holding a device that's recording the mystery of the room. He asks the ghost what he's doing here terrorising the ladies. Nothing. He wants the ghost to touch him. Nothing happens. Momma's spooked by the suspense; she's all jittery with the heebie-jeebies.

If I were the ghost, I'd give the presenter what he wants.

When the show's over, Momma heads upstairs. I rewind the digibox to the credits. Chase – his name is Chase. I rewind some more and now he's splayed across the bed again, all biceps and thighs. I place my cheek on the dusty TV screen and shove a hand down my boxers, willing some supernatural force to take me by the neck and pull me in.

Ballooning

Sylvie hasn't been outside for a week, maybe two. Her husband's bedbound again. She knows Erik can't help it, but still. Dinner needs cooking and there's no food in the house, so he asks her to pop to the shop and grab a few things. He says she can treat him to something sweet to lift his spirits while she's there; he mentions nothing about her spirits.

She isn't going to get a bus into the city. There's a little corner shop at the bottom of the hill. Sylvie's already dreading the walk back up. She folds her tote bag into a tight square and puts it in her coat pocket. One'll be enough. The bag's cream colour is tinged brown from years of reuse, but that's the point. She opens the front door and she didn't realise how stale the air in the house was until she inhaled the afternoon chill.

She closes the front door and leans against it, her back already aching, and admires the view. The hills are lightly dusted with unseasonal snow that has half-melted, and the houses lining her way downhill are uniform yet quaint. The city park is a vast block of green foliage stippled across the middle like a rumour. She always thought this view could be photographed for a postcard, probably already has.

She squints. There's an unbecoming scarlet swelling amongst the greens. She rubs her eyes and sees the hot air balloon inflating. She'd forgotten how big they become. The park's too far off for her to hear the roar of the balloon filling up, but she keeps watching the bright red expanse slowly rise while she walks. She finds herself laughing about the balloon, the way it peeks through the trees like a giant's face. She can't remember the last time she laughed. She sends Erik a text about the hot air balloon, and he asks her to send him a photo.

On her wedding day – so long ago now – Sylvie's mother told her that marriage is all about sacrifice. She remembers this now while watching the hot air balloon rise into the air, strong and with purpose. Watching it floating up through the trees, she almost loses her breath.

She pockets her phone because sometimes there's a little too much sacrifice. She bursts. The hot air balloon rises higher and higher still, and Sylvie waits. The balloon shrinks in the sky, growing smaller the greater their distance becomes. She doesn't dare move until it completely disappears.

Crab Fishing for Sharks

Nella was hesitant about her third date with Jorge. Crab fishing was the last thing she wanted to do. She told him she doesn't like going out of her comfort zone and he tells her that it's crab-fishing, not shark baiting. What Nella meant was that flaccid so-called dates such as crab fishing were out of her comfort zone. Shark baiting sounded great.

Everything on the beach was cold: the barnacled rocks, the sea air, Jorge's knuckles as he gripped the plastic bucket, the way he concentrated his stare on the rock pool, willing his lazy eye to do as it was told.

Nella ripped her cuticles and tore away her skin. She was always picking at her skin, trying to get at what was hidden underneath. Jorge hooked the bait and dropped the line, said nothing.

Out to sea there was an abandoned lighthouse, a relic becoming a ruin. Nella wanted to sail out to it, to dig her fingernails into the lighthouse keeper's old mattress and spend the night making love with his ghost. She wanted to breathe life through the derelict lighthouse walls, she wanted to appear on a TV show as the fixer-upper-of-things that she was. She'd shine a beacon to the world; her light would be her siren song. A man like Jorge would be by her side; groomed, preened, clean and suave. Come here, bring me your problems, I'll fix them.

But she didn't have a boat, and there wasn't any chance she and Jorge would find a shark while crab fishing. Some things can't be saved.

Satsumas

You're peeling a satsuma under a Joshua tree, waiting for him. The rind wedges beneath your fingernails, infusing with the dirt you've forgotten to scrub away. Citrus zests the air. Slowly, half a wedge at a time, you eat the satsuma. Please be careful not to waste any juice. There's the buzzing of cicadas a little way off, but you never cared for the cadence of insects.

The satsuma is of Chinese origin, but was introduced to the west by Japan. Or something like that? The fruit became more common in the United States of America during the nineteenth century. *Citrus unshiu* is a species of citrus fruit that is seedless and easy to peel. The species are also known as *unshu mikan*, cold hardy mandarin, satsuma mandarin, satsuma orange, *nartjie*.

Everyone prefers an easy peel.

Are you easy to peel?

A bundle of satsumas is known as a sweet invigoration, so you brought the satsumas for him. You thought of yourself as sweet and invigorating. Yes, satsumas are nourishing, he said, but they're a commitment, an indulgence not everyone wants to get their teeth into. You bite into your fifth satsuma like an apple; the juice dribbles down your chin, your arms, your wrists.

Seedling

The banner catches Mina's eye. It reads 'The Seeds of Change'. She sees these seeds of change have been sown on a giant block of concrete in the middle of the river, but the plants have been left to rot. Their brittle skeletons stretch up to the sky from terracotta-coloured plastic planters, pleading for sustenance, frozen where they died. She wishes the river was conquerable, something she could swim through so she could hold the plants and nurture them back to health. Only the wind mothers them. Mina closes her eyes and listens to the river, listens for the second heartbeat deep inside her. She knows it's still there despite her worries. She opens her eyes. Green and yellow foliage spill from the planters, purple and orange flowers bloom wide like smiles. Mina barely sees the concrete beneath the unfurling life. Sprouts and saplings are fully grown and blooming. She feels a kick.

MDF

Mother

Romy and his new mum cuddle on her bed while watching *Changing Rooms*. She looks like Linda Barker. His new sister and new dad watch the footie downstairs. Romy says new as if he remembers the old, but he doesn't. He remembers the other orphans told him he wasn't boy enough because he didn't like sports, but he's happiest watching Lawrence Llewelyn-Bowen flounce around and flap about in a panic.

He tugs his mum's dressing gown sleeve and asks if they can go on *Changing Rooms* one day, please? She says, 'Heck no, why would we do that?' She doesn't want her house filled with MDF, she doesn't trust Anna Ryder Richardson not to paint her dining room red.

From downstairs, his dad yells, 'Hang yer fucking cock on that,' which Romy's worked out means a goal has been scored. He doesn't know why you'd want to do that or how doing that would benefit any celebration. He isn't sure what it is you'd be hanging it on either, but his mum turns the telly up like she knows he's about to ask.

Carol Smillie bumbles around a half-painted living-room, distracting Handy Andy from fitting a new door to its frame. Romy wonders if the door's MDF, wonders why anyone would complain about owning a door when he's lived for so long without one of his own.

Daughter

Arabella slams her bedroom door, which could mean any number of things. Romy knows to give his teenage daughter space. She'll come down when her dinner's cold and she'll eat it without reheating. Neither of them will point out the lack of warmth.

Whenever Romy used to get upset, his mum would grin and say, 'Smiley, Smiley, Carol Smillie' until he giggled away the grumps. She'd know how to make his daughter feel better. He should've known better, should've known about all the last times you never knew were coming, all the questions you'd want to ask. He tries to imagine the advice she'd offer and all he can hear is, 'Smiley, Smiley, Carol Smillie.'

He doesn't want to cry because the walls here are thin. His doctor said he's got to cut out coffee because of his heart and he can't imagine decaf can be improved with salt. He's smiling, but if he has to cry he'll do it quietly. He wants to be held, not heard.

Father

Romy fixes the shelves onto the wall while Arabella brings in boxes of clothes from the moving van. He insisted on lending her some of the deposit. What else would he spend the money on?

She comes into the bedroom and heaves a box onto the bed. He asks if she needs a hand bringing anything in and she says, 'No, I'll manage.' He doesn't want her to manage – he wants her to thrive. She stands in the doorway with her arms full of boxes and resolve, and the way she fills the space with resolve reminds Romy of his mum.

'What?' she says. He says nothing.

The doors in this house look like MDF. He'll replace them with new ones. Sturdy, solid oak.

An Ocean Swims Above Our Heads

We're not underwater, we're *under*water. My husband tells me this is the effect the aquarium is going for as if this makes a difference, as if I hadn't reached this conclusion for myself. He wants me to believe this is the same as scuba diving, only safer. He's a cheapskate.

I'm walking through a finger-marked glass tube with too many people, jostling each other and breathing too loud. I can smell clammy skin, I can see body heat lingering on rustling coats. Inauthentic aquatic sounds are being pumped through tinny speakers. We're all under: under water, under a spell, underwhelmed.

He holds my hand because he thinks I'll wander off. That or he loves me. He pulls my arm, wants to get through the aquarium quickly. I resist and take my time. If I can't go diving, then my money's worth.

He feigns enthusiasm and points at a stingray. *That Irwin fella,* he says. I only smile because the stingray itself is striking, carving itself through invisible streams like a graceful bird.

Tropical fish shimmer through rocks and plants. They must miss their home, assuming they know any different. Perhaps it's kinder if they don't know what it's like swimming among dying coral reefs, dodging plastic bags and bottles. They say you can't miss what you've never had but somehow, really, you can. You can miss everything.

People huff. I'm committing one of the cardinal sins of the modern era: I'm standing still in a public place. But I don't want to move. I close my eyes and pretend I'm submerged, that there's no sweaty groups of school children clambering, that the glass tube walls aren't there.

My husband squeezes my hand. I could let go. He could swim the oceans' depth while I barnacle myself here. He squeezes my hand again, firmer this time. It either means I love you or let's get a move on. I don't open my eyes to check which it is.

Her Incarceration

Almost in unison, almost mirrored, they returned their phones to their receivers, their faces solemn. He placed his hand on the glass partition and she aligned her hand to his. Their fingers could not interlock no matter how hard they pressed against the barrier. They'd never touch each other, not for twenty-one years at least. The sallowness of her face alarmed him; it'd only been five weeks. She noticed there were grey hairs scattered in his thinning black mop. They could see the dust gathering all around them, on them. Together they were fading, hoping there'd be something left when their sentence ends.

The Broom of Sisyphus

Dad is outside sweeping fallen leaves from the driveway. Again.

Costume

Breathe in. Breathe out.

I'm alone on the beach I haven't visited in nearly fifty-seven years. The morning sun hasn't triumphed through the clouds, but it's trying to burst through. Everything's murky. I'm perching on the wall that separates the sleeping town from the beach, from the restless sea. Seagulls soar overhead, uncharacteristic in their silent concentration, searching the beach for the dropped chips they've missed from the night before. They hover, the yellow of their beaks cutting the granite sky. I imagine flight and unclipped wings.

I remember the waves and the slippery seaweed beneath them, how they slivered around my ankles and kept me grounded back then. Everything was different in 1907.

Breathe in. Breathe out.

I try to regulate my breathing but it won't calm my nerves. The other women in the beach huts next to mine must be feeling the same. We're sharing the anticipation of what we're about to do.

I drop my robe. Naked shoulders, arms, knees and ankles. Even a little bit of thigh. A black one-piece swimsuit hugs the rest of my body. I'm vulnerable and oddly liberated. Adrenaline kicks in. Fight or flight; whichever it is, it bubbles.

Breathe in. Breathe...

...out, the wind catches the door and I run into sunlight. The beach is full of women like me, running through the sea breeze, smelling excitement and possibility. The sky is cloudless, sanguine. The men call us hussies while we soar. Other women pretend to avert their gaze, feigning disgust for appearance's sake, but they admire us. We laugh at the sun tickling our bare flesh, the waves beckoning us closer.

Breathe. Breathe. Faster. Faster.

With each step I take towards the ocean my fear shrinks into a tiny sphere, a nugget I can cast away in the waves. I taste salt and camaraderie on my tongue. The wind whips past our skin and the sand flicks behind us as we run towards the waves.

The policemens' whistles slices summer, but they can't deafen the freedom our costumes flaunt. They had arrested Annette Kellermann, the Australian professional swimmer, when she wore the same costume we're all wearing now. Men claimed only indecent harlots wear these monstrosities. Why must men claim everything? We knew the police would try to arrest us too, but they had to catch us first.

But they do catch me. They return me to my husband like a lost dog, like a delinquent child.

Breathe in.

Eventually things changed, but my husband didn't. You can't help who you fall in love with; I'd made my vows for better or for worse, and I always held onto the hope that things would get better.

I should've listened to the other women. I should've listened to my gut.

From the beach wall I can see the waves slinking further and further away, but I can still hear their forceful crash on the sand; beating, pounding. After they hit the shore, they caress the sand, soothing and apologetic, but always cold. I hear it whispering: *I'm sorry, I can't help it, you should've done as you were told, my chickadee.*

I rub my arms and legs. The cuts and bruises have faded away but I'm still scarred beneath my black robe. My skin pimples at my own touch, not recognising my own flesh against itself. Sometimes, when I close my eyes, he's there gripping my bones, even though he's gone.

Breathe out.

I leap from the wall and run, letting my black robe fall behind me. It glides through the air before curling into a heap on the sand. I'm naked, wearing only my scars. No costume to hide behind. Slower now, much slower, and everything hurts, but I still feel as young as I was back then. The sun finds its strength and the clouds fade into a jubilant yellow sky. The seagulls' cries grow louder above me, cheering. With my seaweed shackles broken, the ocean welcomes my naked body. Everything isn't exactly weightless and time hasn't quite stood still, but I know I must be finally flying.

Meaning Given, Meaning Found

We walk along the wooden pathways of Red Seabeach, breathing China deep. Crimson reeds glow, waving from the wetland like something fabricated. I want to wave back to check they're real. He and I stand, not speaking. A red-crowned crane swoops and slices the sky, its slender body diving into the scarlet marsh. Is it make believe? The locals tell us those cranes are rare, it's incredible we've seen one. We're fortunate, they say, we're blessed. They're a symbol, those cranes, their appearances signifying good luck, fidelity, and longevity. I squeeze his hand, hoping we'll have no use for charms.

Brass Door Handles, Rose Petals, Money Spider

The brass handles on the double-doors look polished but they aren't. There's a smudginess to them. A child with sticky hands must've touched them and the residue has been allowed to dry. Dangling beneath the left handle is a cobweb, loose and thick and almost floating. Roxanne often wonders about the difference between cobwebs and spider webs, still isn't sure what the distinction is. She scans for a spider, but her concern is fleeting. She concentrates on her own reflection; warped, bending in the mucky caramel to form some kind of monster. Nausea. She wobbles on the spot, the earth moving beneath her feet. She cannot see her shoes, but knows the nude heels are cutting deep. There'll be a blister – bright orange and new. Still, she focuses on those brass door handles to distract herself from what's about to happen. Those dirty-gold oblongs boasting hungry keyholes framed by vines. They are faces, watching her; there will be more faces, and they'll be watching her soon. She grips her bouquet of roses as if they're anchoring her to the ground. She can't smell them. Her father's arm loops in hers, accompanied by his potent aftershave – cinnamon infused gasoline. In her mouth, tension salivates copper. Her skin itches in the only dress she could find that hadn't made her look like a dumpling-shaped whip of shaving foam. She feels the weight of it all. She breathes, knowing that he's going to be standing there on the other side of the door. The bridal party gather behind her. Her father says something, she thinks. Smile, she tells herself, just smile. She does and nods, unsure if he asked her if she's ready. He lifts her veil. The world as seen through her veil offers brief security before she must walk through those doors. They reach for the handles and she wants to find a sanitary wipe so she can clean their hands. The pipe-organ bellows, and she stares at her bouquet, the rose petals, her fingertips. Anything but their eyes – their unwelcome, searching eyes.

Church organs dig their fingers into the air and pry it apart, filling the church with its deep groan. The doors open, the congregation stand, and Lloyd turns around like he's supposed to, like they rehearsed. It's like following a script. Smile, he tells himself, just smile to the congregation while time slows, while she walks step-by-step-by-step, like a mist drifting in. What is it they say about brides, that they're glowing and radiant? Or is that pregnant women? Concentrate on her bouquet. Petals like velvet, petals fresh and alive but dying. He cannot see their thorns through the peach ribbon, but he can see the white of her fingernails where she's gripping the bouquet tightly. He looks down at his shoes, the black leather shining, and he wishes his shoes would grow toward his shins, his knees, his thighs, then consume him entirely. He knows he should be looking at her, but he admires the stained-glass windows. He wants to touch the saints and their stories, he wants to feel the greens and blues and reds and know what morals they're both supposed to uphold. She's much closer now, and he can smell those flowers too. He looks at the bouquet again, and he can see the tiny limbs of a money spider dancing among those red and pink petals. Money spiders are supposed to represent fortune, but the unmistakable scent of decay laces the roses. The money spider doesn't care about the smell. It weaves its web between two roses, thin yet taut, as if it will hold all of this together. Though the organ blares, he can only hear her heels stabbing the stone slabs, a steady rhythm that clacks no comfort. Her dress trails over etchings marking the tombs of the dead underfoot, and he looks for dust clinging to the rim of her dress. Anything to not look at her, but then he does because that's what's expected of him, because otherwise people will start speculating, because she's standing right in front of him now and how can he not look. The white veil is patterned with roses, their petals falling. He lifts her veil over her hair and she's crying. Not tumultuous tears that steal her makeup as they snake their way down her face, but the quiet, unfallen crying that pools at the base of the eye and waits, like rainwater caught in a petal with nowhere to run. He doesn't understand this happiness of hers but, despite it all, she's never looked more ravishing. He won't ruin this for her.

They both say I do even though they don't.

A Husband for Hire

Sophie considers the Facebook advert at length. There were benefits to owning a husband of your own, but a rental would provide her with better flexibility and more options. They could come and go as she pleases. She clicks through to the Husbands4Hire website.

The company is well-reviewed, and the husbands provide a wide range of services: repairs, painting and decorating, plumbing, electrical, garden landscaping, and more. Husbands4Hire list everything they believe a woman couldn't do or shouldn't have to do. Men, apparently, could do it all – for a price.

Not all men. Sophie found the list of services limited and unimaginative. She could think of many other ways a husband may prove useful.

Deciding there was still something empowering about hiring men to do your bidding, she phones Husbands4Hire. Her hired husband would arrive in approximately twenty-five minutes, maybe thirty. It could be fun, an experiment of sorts. A white van pulls up on Sophie's driveway and she peeks through the letterbox before opening the front door.

The husband for hire is tool-belted and tall, with a stocky, steady build and a face as smooth as he'll promise your walls. He's prematurely pot-bellied and balding but in a way she found somewhat attractive, and faded tattoos crawl up his left arm. It would be difficult for her to make out what the tattoos were unless he came closer.

"What's your name?"

"Dave."

Dave. A sturdy, dependable Dave. A perfect name for a husband. She invited him in, and he looked around, quietly assessing her immaculate home. He asks who did her bathroom grouting and she tells him she did it herself.

"But what work needs doing?" he asks, following her into the bedroom. "There's nothing here that needs fixing?"

Men can be so silly, always trying to fix everything. Sophie closes the bedroom door.

Spotting

It's him. He's lifting weights, wearing that red football shirt he always wore. It can't be the same shirt he used to wear at school under his sweater, but it's fun to pretend. The gym mirror reflects my early-onset bad-bod while I run on the treadmill. Now he has tacky tribal tattoos and a chiselled face. The muscles are new, too. But those eyes are the same. Pale-green innocence. Eyes that make girls swoon. Some girls. Not only girls. He spots me watching him in the mirror and winks.

I'm fifteen. My face is pockmarked and full of holes. He calls me, Crumpet. He pushes me to the ground, spits on my face. He calls me…He calls me a faggot. Fairy. Puffter. Nancy. Gaylord. He does the same to Hamish too, even though he's straight. Guys like him never see the harm in it. Guys like him never see.

The guy in the red football shirt winks again, acting like we're cool. We're not cool; if his vanity asks me to spot him, I'll let the weight of it all crush his windpipe.

Lemons, All Slightly Shrivelled...

...a lone lime, a small jug of water, a paring knife, a blue and white check porcelain bowl, two foggy glasses scratched by time, a wooden chopping block well-worn from years of shared use, a blue tablecloth with gold polka dots, two oak chairs – one a little rickety with an elderly woman sitting on it, the other empty. The elderly woman, her hands always trembling these days, picks up the knife, the lime, and slices. She scrapes the lime into the small jug of water. Droplets plop and spring, zest and juice infuse. There's a knock on the door. The elderly woman rises, steadies herself on the table, and tightens the shawl draped over her shoulders. She opens the door to the Tuscan sun and another elderly woman, her friend. Her third friend today. They all come out to visit her now. They kiss each other's cheeks, and the elderly woman welcomes her friend inside. The elderly woman tells her friend not to remove her shoes, but the friend insists on doing so, says it's respectful to the dead. Not to my nose, the elderly woman thinks. She offers her friend a glass of water with lime, but her friend asks if she could have lemon instead, says she prefers the zing of a lemon to a zang of a lime. The elderly woman shakes her head, refuses to touch the lemons. She tells her friend that the lemons were his, are his. A lemon tumbles from the bowl and rolls to the edge of the table. See, the elderly woman shouts so any who desire lemons may hear, he's still here, still watching his lemons. Her friend takes the knife and cuts the runaway lemon into slices. He's gone, she says, and the friends embrace, both quietly crying.

Yellow

They're lying in bed together when she asks him, "Will you still love me when I'm yellow?"

"When you're yellow?"

"Yes, when I'm yellow."

He has no idea what she's talking about, but she's gripping the duvet and won't look him in the eye, so he knows she's being serious. He squeezes her closer to him, his hand resting on her upper arm, near the sickle-shaped scar he likes to trace with his too-long index finger.

"Are you turning yellow then?"

"Does it matter?" She sits up and reaches for her book.

It shouldn't matter but it does, he thinks. He imagines her yellow, her ballerina limbs stretching margarine sunshine across the stage. They'd call her the yellow swan. He imagines her jaundiced and in hospital, he imagines her dying. He stops, forces himself to think about what is actually happening rather than what isn't.

It's either too late at night or too early in the morning for a conversation like this. Time's something he's always forgetting about around her, isn't something he remembers to measure. But she's waiting for an answer and, whatever the time is, he knows he's kept her waiting too long.

"Alright," he says, "I'll still love you when you're yellow."

In the bathroom, she checks her hands, her skin, the whites of her eyes to see if she's turning yellow. She knows she isn't, but she still likes to check. Knowing for certain helps her sleep.

She slides back into bed, clambers over him and rests across his legs. He tries easing her off, but she doesn't budge. She bats away his arms when he tries to tickle her, both of them chirruping like canaries in the dim light. They stop. She holds his face in her hands like a mango she's scared to bruise. Neither blinks.

"You have to promise me," she whispers. "Do you promise?"

He doesn't care what time it is, he has all the time in the world for this.

"Sure," he says, "I promise I'll still love you when you're yellow. When you're blue, when you're green, purple, orange, red –"

She pulls the duvet over them both.

Curving the Pointy Edges

Hector pulls all the furniture in the house away from the walls by six inches. He wants to tease his wife, he wants to wind her up for no reason. When Niamh comes home, she plays along and makes no comment about the furniture. She reclines on the sofa and asks him if he'd mind rubbing her shoulders.

"I can only rub your shoulders with my left hand. I forgot to wear gloves in the garden this afternoon and nicked my other hand on several thorns."

He rubs her shoulders with both hands anyway. She doesn't tell him to stop.

This morning, they woke up with the torn-out pages of a *Learn to Speak French in a Year* calendar scattered around them. They threw the pages into the air and danced together in their underwear. Tomorrow they are flying out for their second shot at a honeymoon. First Paris, then a Scandinavian tour.

There are freshly cut roses in a vase on the dining table that Niamh didn't spot when she came in. The petals are a dark, deep red, almost purple, and she has no intention of mentioning them.

On the plane, Niamh tells Hector that she used to be a casting director. She's never told him this before. It was her way of turning her unintentional habit of judging people into an employable skill. She made them all stars in her day. He asks her what role she would cast him in, what kind of film, what kind of star she'd make of him.

"I'd cast us in a timeless classic," she says and climbs into his lap. "A romance where nothing bad ever happens." She then lowers her voice to a whisper. "We'd be the brightest of stars."

Their noses are touching when an air stewardess reminds Niamh that the pilot has switched on the seatbelt light and she should please return to her seat while they prepare to land. Niamh does as she's told, but not before she gets what she wants.

Hector wakes up on their second morning in Paris with a stye, his right eyelid puffy like a blood orange segment. Niamh pulls him on top of her and tells him to fuck her. He hovers above her, doesn't speak. He tries not to look away but he's shaking, he's quivering all over. Lost, he kisses her forehead and pulls away. She slaps his arm – part playful, part pissed – brings him a soggy teabag, and presses it gently over his stye. "It'll be gone in a week," she says, "maybe sooner."

Later they dance above the city skyline. Niamh's white feather boa trails across the Eiffel Tower's viewing platform, a pendulum of pearls draped around her neck. People watch them glide as if they're in a movie, as if they're woeless lovers sharing their first dance.

Scandinavia is colder than they thought. Doubtful they'll ever see the Northern Lights, they quarrel as they wade through the snow. Niamh sifts through pine needles, unsure of what she's searching for, while Hector traces his thoughts in fireplace ash.

In Helsinki, Niamh decides she wants to become a glassblower. When they return home, she'll find the nearest course at a college and study part time.

"We need our own outlets, something we can focus on that isn't each other," Niamh tells him, "something that isn't about what happened to us."

Hector pulls her close. His landscaping business isn't doing well enough for her to drop her hours down, but he agrees with her. They'll find a way to make everything work.

Three years after the night they danced above Paris, Niamh is comparing iceberg lettuces at the farmers market when she swoons. Hector catches her while lettuces roll down the cobbled streets. After the doctor's appointment, they unpack dusty boxes filled with cupboard locks and maternity clothes. They bubble-wrap each other, stick cotton wool on the walls, curve all the pointy edges. When their daughter is born, they give her a different name every week until a year passes: Hope, Prue, Libby, Faith, Florence, Joy... They settle on Evangeline, after Niamh's grandmother who promised them that things always look worse than they are. They hold each other close so they can't be snatched away.

The Moon is a Foreign Body, We Can No Longer Trust It

Following the will of the people, the government decide to nuke the moon. A little over half of the world's population succumbed to the rhetoric spread across social media by overnight experts and algorithms. Some people believe the moon is the source of all their worldly problems and it'd be for the best if the moon was gone. *The moon is a drain on our society. The moon is causing climate change. No longer will the Earth be a slave to this satellite.* They became suspicious of the moon, who'd always been there watching over us.

Despite the protests, despite the petitions and the marches, the government said we had a vote, that this was the result, and it would be undemocratic not to follow the will of the people. *We are nuking the moon. We are going to make our planet great again! We are taking back control of our tides! This will be our defining moment in history – why would we need to double-check something so momentous?*

They televise the detonation, but you don't tune in. You don't want to watch the nuking of the moon. You're one of the voters from the other half, the half who listened to the scientists and their evidence, who read the reports detailing exactly what would happen if we nuked the moon.

Unfortunately, you have no choice but to watch the moon explode.

The sky lights up while you're driving down the motorway, uncertain of where you were going, of where you could now go. It's impossible not to hear the sky crack, to see a vista become violent, red, orange, and angry. A skyscape of mistakes, an irreparable permanence. You pull over and vomit, you wipe your mouth and beard on your sleeve and stare up as streaks of purple fire carve the sky. Everything's sweltering, as if nothing will ever be cold again.

Soon, pieces of the moon will pummel the earth. The moon was born of the earth, and so it would return. Ashes to ashes, dust to dust. Without the gravitational pull of the moon, the earth will tilt. For years the remnants of the moon will twirl in orbit, eventually forming a shimmering ring. You'd love to see this ring, can imagine it to be the only wonderous outcome of this mess, but you know you never will live to see this ring glisten.

You stretch across your car bonnet, the chance we all had to change our minds smouldering into the metal. You close your eyes, you breathe slow and deep, and you wait for pieces of the moon to decide what will happen to you next.

Acknowledgements

This Alone Could Save Us would not have been possible without the love and support of so many. My unreserved gratitude goes to everyone who helped bring this book into existence, especially:

Jude Higgins at Ad Hoc Fiction, for her belief in these words and for everything she does for the flash fiction community; John at Ad Hoc Fiction, for his book production wizardry; Diane Simmons, for her hawk-eye proofreading abilities; my fellow National Flash Fiction Day Co-Directors, Diane Simmons and Ingrid Jendrzejewski, for allowing me to take a year off which allowed the time to work on this collection; and Stuart Buck, for kindly allowing me to use his stunning artwork for the cover.

Thank you to Angela Readman, Diane Simmons, Kathy Fish, Meg Pokrass, Robert Scotellaro, and Vanessa Gebbie, who kindly carved time away from their own projects to read and provide generous thoughts about this book.

To my friends and family for their constant love, support, and tolerance.

To Matthew, for everything he does and for everything he is.

Previously Published

Grateful acknowledgement is made to the following anthologies and journals in which these pieces appeared in an earlier form:

Full Circle – *And Other Poems*

The Greatest Temptation of Mother Teresa – *Spelk*

Dissolve – *MoonPark Review; Best Microfiction 2020*

Tessellation – *Unbroken Journal*

Showering – *Flash: The International Short-Short Story Magazine* – Issue 11.2

The Landmines Up Near Sapper Hill Sing – *FlashBack Fiction*

Because We All Need the Snow – *FlashFlood*

Nonni – *Ripening: National Flash Fiction Day Anthology 2018*, edited by Santino Prinzi and Alison Powell

Towels – *With One Eye on the Cows: Bath Flash Fiction Volume Four*

This Way Around – *With One Eye on the Cows: Bath Flash Fiction Volume Four*

Upon Discovering that Cows Can Swim – *Jellyfish Review; The Best Small Fictions 2019*, edited by Nathan Leslie and Rilla Askew

You Lost Something in Your Earthquake that You'll Never Get Back – *The Lobsters Run Free: Bath Flash Fiction Volume Two*

Getting the Gang Back Together – *Flash: The International Short-Short Story Magazine* – Issue 10.1

Her Incarceration – *Long Exposure Magazine*

MDF – *And We Pass Through: National Flash Fiction Day Anthology 2019,* edited by Santino Prinzi and Joanna Campbell

The Broom of Sisyphus – *Micro Madness: National Flash Fiction Day New Zealand*, First Place Winning Micro

Meaning Given, Meaning Found – *100 Word Story*

Spotting – *Ellipsis Zine*

Lemons, All Slightly Shrivelled… – *Flash: The International Short-Short Story Magazine* – Issue 11.2

Curving the Pointy Edges – *SmokeLong Quarterly*

About the Author

Santino Prinzi is a Co-Director of National Flash Fiction Day in the UK, is one of the founding organisers of the annual Flash Fiction Festival, and is a Consulting Editor for *New Flash Fiction Review.* He writes flash fiction, prose poetry, and is currently working on a novel.

His flash fiction pamphlet, *There's Something Macrocosmic About All of This* (2018), is available from V. Press, and his short flash collection, *Dots and other flashes of perception* (2016), is available from The Nottingham Review Press. His work has been selected for the *Best Small Fictions 2019* and *Best Microfiction 2020* anthologies, and he has received nominations for the Best of the Net, the Pushcart Prize, and the Best British and Irish Flash Fiction. His stories have been published in *SmokeLong Quarterly, Flash: The International Short-Short Story Magazine, Jellyfish Review,* 100-*Word Story,* Bath Flash Fiction Award anthologies, National Flash Fiction Day anthologies, Reflex

Fiction, and others. He has also contributed an academic chapter about Franz Kafka and Robert Walser to *Critical Insights: Flash Fiction,* which is available from Grey House Publishing (2017).

To find out more, follow him on Twitter (@ tinoprinzi) or visit his website: santinoprinzi.com